Kunyi

For my children – Yaritji, Ribnga,
Kamara, and Gail-Daisy

Kunyi

Kunyi June Anne McInerney

These are my stories from a dry remote place, where growing up was very different from what Australian children know today.

I was born in Todmorden Station near Oodnadatta in South Australia. My mother was a Yankunytjatjara woman, and she named me Kunyi.

My mother worked on the station as a domestic servant, and my granny looked after me. I have many memories of us children helping our grannies in the camp; sometimes to collect firewood to keep warm, or to boil a billy, or to cook.

Our grannies told us stories around the campfire. Their stories were about a lesson to be learned. This is how we were taught to respect country and to know the laws. My granny only spoke her Yankunytjatjara language.

Our people lived in camps nearby, and our homes were humpies made of corrugated tin collected from the dump. We used potato-sack bags to fill the gaps in the walls and to line the dirt floors. In those days, Aboriginal people did not live in houses unless they were married to a European person.

When I was four years old, I was taken to live with the missionaries at the Oodnadatta Children's Home run by the United Aborigines Mission. They called me 'Anne' and told me to speak English. My younger brothers and sister, Thomas, Michael and Robyn, were also taken. The Children's Home became our home, and the other children became our only family.

From that time on, we only saw the life that should have been ours by looking out towards our camps on the other side of the railway line. Because of government policy, some kids with darker skin were allowed to stay with their families. They learned Yankunytjatjara way.

If our families built their camps too close to the mission, Sergeant Evans made them move to the other side of Oodnadatta so he could keep his eye on them from the police station. There was a big fence along that road. Our people weren't allowed to walk around town, and most of the day they sat under the shade of two big trees.

I am telling my story now so that our lives at the Children's Home will not be forgotten.

Kunyi June Anne McInerney

KJM

The Oodnadatta Children's Home

It was nighttime when we arrived at the Oodnadatta Children's Home. We didn't really understand how we got there. The older children told us that a policeman brought us in. There were kids of all ages already there. Sister Bullpit and her assistant, Sister Kotz, were in charge of us.

The Children's Home was run by the United Aborigines Mission. The mission house was just a corrugated iron shed with no insulation. We soon discovered it was really hot in summer and cold in winter. The dining area was at the front under the verandah – the boys sat on the left and the girls on the right. We slept in two separate dormitories, which were behind the dining area. Behind the main house was the mission classroom, which doubled as the visitors' house.

dormitory life

There were six bunk-beds in the girls' dormitory. If there were more kids than bunks, we slept two to a bed.

On hot nights, the missionaries made the boys carry our beds outside. Dingoes would come in from the desert plains and hang around the mission house. They usually moved away when our dog, Kim, barked. I remember one night when the dingoes were howling, and the wind was blowing. We could see scary shapes in the trees, and were so scared the boys had to put our beds back inside.

washing sheets

Our bed sheets were rags, and I had three or four strips of rags across my bed. The first night at the home, I woke up in the morning to a wet bed. I wet my bed for a long time after that. Right from the start, I was up before sunrise to wash the rags. Instead of washing them in the house laundry, I had to walk across to the visitors' laundry. I was scared of the dark, and it felt like all the bushes and trees made noises. The laundry trough was high, and I stood on a box to reach it. I always cried a lot waiting for the sun to come up.

Every morning, all the kids filed out of the dormitory to empty their potties in a toilet pit far away from the mission house. It was still dark, and we could barely see the ground. While they were out, the missionaries placed undies, dresses and pants in rows on the end of each bed.

sneaking books

Outside the dormitory door was a bookshelf. If we were sent to bed early, the older girls would sneak books as we weren't allowed to read them. Sister Bullpit slept in a room across from the dormitory, and my bunk was in line with her bed. If she was lying facing me, I'd whisper, 'She's looking this way.' If she turned away, I'd tell the girls the coast was clear. One girl would crawl to the doorway, reach around and grab a book for the oldest girl to read. If she'd already read it, another girl had to go back, grab a different one and return the first book. If the girl dropped the book, she'd crawl backwards to her bed.

If we got a book without being caught, the oldest girl would whisper the story to us. Sister Bullpit was always listening though. 'Anne, what's going on?' she'd yell. 'Nothing!' I'd call back.

playing with the lamp

There was no electricity and we used a kerosene lamp. If the missionaries had visitors and were talking outside, or had gone to sleep, Dotty would dance around the lamp to make us laugh. I was scout and if I saw Sr Bullpit coming, we all jumped back into bed. We dived under the covers and pretended to be asleep.

I remember the nights we played daredevil with a large centipede. In the lamplight, we could see it running around the floor. We hung our heads over the edge of the bottom bunks until the centipede got close to our faces – then we quickly lifted our heads up. Everyone burst out laughing as each girl missed the centipede by a fraction.

Dotty Khan was the main girl who danced. She made us laugh a lot.

All the girls shared the same bathwater. The youngest ones bathed first, all in together. I never saw a bath with clean water at the Children's Home – we didn't know anything different. We had fun, though, wetting each other and rinsing our soapy hair in the dirty water.

washing our hair

The missionaries cut our hair, and we all looked like we had bowls on our heads. If our hair ever grew long enough, the older girls or the missionaries tied it up with ribbons.

If one person got head lice, everyone had to have kerosene put through their hair and then have it washed out with Velvet Soap.

kitchen work

All the children had to work. Boxes of fruit and vegetables arrived on the train from Adelaide and were delivered on the back of the ute. Us girls worked on the verandah sorting food for the storeroom. Then we started peeling. I peeled potatoes. One girl peeled pumpkins, and one carrots. Other girls shelled peas and chopped the cabbage. The missionaries growled us if we were slow and said things like 'No talking!'

The wood stove heated the top plate and the oven, and the boys collected wood for the stove and laundry copper. The copper boiled water to wash the clothes.

We weren't allowed in the kitchen unless the missionaries were in a good mood. Only then would they show us what they were cooking. When they baked, it was the girls who handed the cakes around to the visitors. Sister Isabelle baked the cakes, and she only liked the boys. No matter how much we asked, only the boys got the cakes.

meal times

All our meals began by singing grace. We weren't allowed to leave the table until everyone had eaten, but the bathroom was behind the girls' table and sometimes we snuck out to get a drink from the tap.

While we ate, we looked out for dust on the track leading from Macumba Station, hoping it was one of our family coming to visit. One time, the truck stopped between the dump and the mission, and my mother walked out from behind the truck. 'It's Auntie Daisy!' everyone else yelled. I had to be calm or else I'd get pinched real hard, jealous-way, by the other kids. After we'd finished eating, my sister Robyn and I sat with our mother on a long seat by the fence.

If we ate late, it got so dark on the verandah that we couldn't see across the plains. That's when the older kids scared us by talking about Mamu (bad spirits). We always ate fast to get back to the dormitory.

At breakfast, the big kids would get the little ones to put flies in someone's porridge. If the little ones said anything, they got kicked under the table or had their hair pulled. Once the big kids did it to my little sister, and I yelled at them. When the missionaries found out what was going on they made the culprits eat the porridge, and they never did it again.

KJM

Once the 'devil' came in – a snake slid through the doorway and under a chair. 'Wamı!' yelled the boys. Sister Bullpit didn't know what was going on. She yelled at everyone to sit down, but us kids ran outside to the sandpit while the older boys got rid of the snake.

Bible lessons

Morning and night, we had Bible lessons. We sang hymns accompanied by Sister Bullpit on the piano accordion. She told us stories from the Old Testament, using cloth figures of people, donkeys and camels on a felt board. Sister Bullpit was always careful to reveal the characters slowly as she told the story. We sat on little carpet squares and, if we didn't pay attention, we had to stand in a corner or spend the next Saturday afternoon on our beds.

preaching at sunrise

I remember the time Sister Bullpit dragged us up before sunrise. She loaded us onto the ute, and we drove to a hill past Hookey's Hole. It was dark and cold, and we walked up that hill with no shoes on. We were terrified of snakes, spiders, centipedes, scorpions and dingoes, but worst of all, Mamu. Sister Bullpit preached, and we just wanted to go back to bed.

Sunday church

Most of the families came to our church on Sunday. It was not really a church – more of a gathering place under a tree outside the mission – but it made us happy to see our family. We sat in the sandpit, or on mats, and sang 'Jesus Loves Me This I Know' in our Yankunytjatjara language.

We were allowed to sing in language because our people were there. Other times, we talked in language away from the missionaries in places where they couldn't hear us.

I was so excited when my Granny Tjandi (Sandy) turned up. I sat next to her, and she wrapped her arms around me. It was a loving, caring feeling that I didn't get from the missionaries. When Granny left, I hid behind the butterfly bush next to the forbidden garden of prickly roses and cried. Sister Kotz yelled out, 'Who is crying? Crying like a baby, you will be treated like a baby!' She made me wear a nappy, but Sister Bullpit told her to take it off and then sent me off to play.

KJM

what we treasured

One day, the missionaries asked some of our mothers to take us out. There was my mother Daisy, Aunty Mary Carol, and Aunty Bibi McCallum. It was one of only four times I saw my mother at the Children's Home. That's why I remember it so well. We went to the dump to find treasures, but we cried on the way because the gibber stones were hot. Our mothers had to tie cardboard around our feet. Those cardboard shoes stayed on until we begged piggyback rides from the older girls.

making toys

We didn't have toys to play with – we made our own. The boys found old tyres and rolled them across the paddock, the tyres in front making tracks for those behind. They stacked the tyres and then pulled tin across the top to make cubby houses. They'd see who had the highest cubby and then climb in. Sometimes there were two or three boys in a stack. If the missionaries yelled at us for bringing stuff home, the boys had to roll their tyres back to the dump.

We only had tin plates and cups at the home, so we girls treasured the broken crockery cups, plates and teapots we found. We looked for pretty ones decorated with pictures of roses, and women in puffy dresses and bonnets in horse-drawn carriages. We hid our treasures under the water tank, or buried them in the dirt with bits of broken glass on top. It was exciting to see where our treasures were hiding.

The boys collected milk cans. They filled them with sand and threaded wire through the middle. The cans turned like wheels and made tracks as they rolled noisily over the gibber stones. The best cans were the Sunshine Milk ones. The babies were given Sunshine Milk so the boys always had lots of cans to play with.

patterns and colours

Church groups in Adelaide often sent us clothes and fabric squares. The missionaries gave us the fabric to play with, and we were in awe of the pretty patterns and colours. We laid them out as if they were beautiful sheets for beds in our imaginary houses, or we piled them up to make dolls' beds, even though we had no dolls.

Sunday art

Every Sunday after lunch, we had a nap – even during the school holidays. Afterwards, the missionaries brought out boxes of pencils and paper. First, we were told a Bible story and we then had to draw what we remembered. I pestered the older kids to draw me pictures of trees and rivers, but they made me do my own. It was the first time I had used pencils and paper.

We also painted with watercolour, and moulded shapes of people, animals and trees out of plasticine. Every Sunday was different – it was up to the missionaries what we were allowed to do. This was where I learned to draw and paint. I have been painting ever since.

bush trips

Sometimes, the missionaries took us out on the ute for picnics. We drove east to the Simpson Desert and saw desert quails, or south to the big bridges about sixty miles away. Only the older boys were allowed to walk over them – the rest of us were too scared anyway. We had more fun jumping between the sticky clay mounds and making tracks in the bog. If the ute got bogged on the way home, we all had to jump out and push.

wildflowers

After the rain, we drove out to see the wildflowers. The daisies looked like a desert carpet, and the earth smelled like perfume.

We played a game to see who would be the first one to see certain flowers. Peggy, the oldest girl, liked the yellow buttercups but the malu kuru (kangaroo eyes) were my favourite. They brightened up the desert. We all wanted to be the first to see the malu kuru and would scream if we spotted one. If the missionaries stopped to let us pick them, we held the flowers against our skin. Malu kuru are the only flowers that feel cool in the desert heat.

sucking bone marrow

Whenever we were out in the bush, the boys looked for animal bones. They smashed them with rocks so we could suck on the bone marrow. That marrow was delicious.

gibber stones

We had a lot of fun walking everywhere. We went to the waterholes at Hookey's Hole and Angle Pole, to the dump and the sandhills, and to the creek under the train-line. Angle Pole is where the old telegraph line changed direction from heading north and went west.

Going to the dump, we'd always try to walk on the dry, weedy grass because the ground and gibber stones in front of the mission were stinking hot under our bare feet. Gibbers are stones that have been baked by the sun and polished by hot winds blowing over the sand.

Hookey's Hole

swimming

Hookey's Hole was one of the favourite places. One time, when Sister Bullpit and Sister Kotz were away, the relief missionaries sent us there for the day. It was a long walk in the sun – about six kilometres – but it was a place where we could have fun and talk in our own language without being told off. To get there, we walked along the dirt track next to the airport, laughing and screaming as the galahs, cockies and crows screeched in the trees close by.

We'd already have our bathers on, and we hung our clothes on big tree roots that stuck out of the water. The creek was always full so we dived off the roots like it was a diving board, or jumped straight in. One time, I came up gasping for air and, after that, I felt safer just sitting on the roots and dangling my feet.

bush tucker

After a while, Peggy would order everyone out of the water to look for bush tucker. We were lucky if we found tiny, sweet onion bulbs and not so lucky if they were old and chalky. We also loved to eat the sweet sticky, gum from the gum trees.

There were hundreds of trees on both sides of the creek at Hookey's Hole, and there was a little island in the middle. We would try to climb the different gum trees. The boys would climb high in the branches to look for honey grubs on the gum leaves. If they found galah and cocky eggs, we ate them raw! The boys would slingshot cockies with their homemade shanghais. There was hardly any meat, but we still made a fire and cooked them. We just sucked on the bones – they were delicious.

If the mangata tree was loaded with mangata (wild peaches), we took some back to the mission for the oldest girl to stew. Whatever we found, we shared.

KJM

KJ.M

the safety tree

Some days, stockmen rode past with bullocks from the cattle yards. The bullocks had come off the train the day before. After they were branded, the stockmen drove them to one of the stations. If we heard the bullocks coming, we climbed up a special tree. That tree was our safety tree. Each kid always sat in the same spot. Even today, I can name all the kids in that tree. I'm on the lowest fork on the left with my cousin, Tjumi. The stockmen were related to some of the kids and gave them lollies to share.

walking in the dark

When it was time to leave, the bigger kids hurried us up. 'Mamu's under the water and will grab you. We not gunna see you anymore,' they'd cry out. We ran so fast that sometimes we forgot our clothes. If we got tired, the older kids gave us piggybacks. Everyone knew snakes slept in the heat of the day, but we still looked out for them as well as for dingoes, camels and cheeky cows.

One night, we got into big trouble after leaving some clothes behind. The missionaries sent us back to get them. It was pitch black, and we ran silently along the track and across the creeks. The bushes and trees at the airport fence looked scary in the shadows, and everyone encouraged each other. If we strayed off the track, the older ones called out, 'Mamu behind you!'

Our people who lived not far from the track were sitting by their campfires. They saw us and yelled at us to go back, but we knew we'd be punished if we didn't find the clothes.

Suddenly, there was a huge beam of light shining down in front of us. I got a big fright. We wouldn't have found our clothes without that big light. We never forgot how it showed us the way. We got back to the mission just as the sun was rising. The missionaries must have been feeling guilty because they were very happy to see us. We didn't tell them about the light – they wouldn't have believed us.

dugka dugka

Another time, we heard the 'dugka dugka' on the way home from Hookey's Hole. It was the cart on the train-line. The other kids ran to the track, but I was too tired. The cart stopped to pick us up, and they all yelled for me to hurry up. Luckily, the driver waited and the girls pulled me on. We got off at Oodnadatta and walked the rest of the way home. The missionaries never found out about our ride on the dugka dugka.

Repeat 'dugka dugka . . . dugka dugka' a few times and you will hear the rhythm and sound of the cart. It's a name we kids made up.

claypans and sandhills

When we went to the claypans between the sandhills, there was one sandhill covered in a vine with big spiky prickles. Only the southern part of the sandhill had the vine, but the missionaries made us walk that way. They drove in the ute and met us on the other side. The older kids walked ahead and tried to get us to step in their footprints, but we still got prickles in our feet.

Wave patterns made by the wind crisscrossed the sand. We drew our own patterns with sticks and our fingers. Down the sand-dunes we rolled – somersaulting and doing acrobatic tricks, playing hide-and-seek and chasey.

Sometimes there were organised games like sack and running races, or apples dangling on a string. You had to try and eat the apple blindfolded with your hands behind your back. I could never do it.

At the bottom of the big sandhill was a claypan. On hot days, it was covered in delicate mosaic patterns. As we raced over it, the clay crackled and turned to fine sand. After the rain, the clay was soggy and stuck to our feet.

games

One of our favourite games was knucklebones. We collected the knucklebones from the carcasses of animals like kangaroos or dingoes, and we played that game for hours.

Marbles was also fun, although we had arguments or fights if someone was found cheating. Mostly, the missionaries made the boys play at the front of the mission and the girls in the sandpit.

mani mani

The missionaries got people to bring in river-sand so we could have a sandpit. The girls' favourite game in the sandpit was 'mani mani', a game with gum leaves – 'big leaf' is the father, 'middle leaf' is the mother, and 'little leaf' is the child. We sat in a circle and placed our leaves down as we told our story. When the story was finished, we started another one with fresh leaves.

We also drew baby animal tracks in the sand – kalaya (emu), malu (kangaroo), wami (snake) – and iti (baby human). As we talked, we drew their tracks.

We played these games nearly every day because everyone wanted to tell a story. Sometimes they were funny, and sometimes they were serious. When the missionaries weren't around, the older girls told their stories in our language. Our grannies had told us stories this way while drawing in the soft creek sand.

KJM

animals and pets

At a certain time of the year – I don't remember when – there would be thousands of beautiful orange and black butterflies fluttering around the flowers on the bush next to the sandpit. My friend Tjumi and I still talk about those butterflies.

After the rain, we hunted for strange insects and frogs in the puddles and ponds. The boys chased us with scorpions and centipedes clinging onto their sticks.

The best one was the 'debil-debil' (devil-devil lizard). They are spiky and beautiful, and they never bit us. The boys collected flies and ants and any other insects they could find to feed them. We kept those lizards in the dining room, but they always seemed to escape back into the desert.

the lone camel

One day, a lone camel came over the train line and up the dirt track in front of the Children's Home. We thought it was coming into the yard and we got really scared. Tjumi held on to our pet joey, called Joey, and one of the boys kept an eye on our dog, Kim. But the camel went around the front fence and past the swing to the station houses.

desert shrimps

After a big rain, desert shrimps would come out of the mud. We would collect them up in our hands. They had a hard shell on the top. I don't think you could eat them. We didn't. When it was dry, we never saw them.

galloping brumbies

One time, driving back from Angle Pole swimming hole, we saw brumbies galloping down the road. We beat them to the turn-off to Oodnadatta and then they passed us. It was beautiful to see their manes fly free. We fought over the different horses as if they were our own – 'That horse is mine!' or 'You can have that old brown one.'

Cocky

Tjumi had a pet cocky given to her by someone in her family. Cocky sat on your shoulder and copied what you were saying. The boys taught him to swear in our Yankunytjatjara language. When the missionaries growled at us, Cocky would screech out swear words and we would burst out laughing. I don't ever remember that cocky in a cage. He was around for a long time.

visit by Uncle and his horse

Uncle Hughie (my mother's younger brother) came to the Children's Home on his horse. He lifted me up onto the saddle, but I didn't want to be on the horse. It was too big. All the kids were watching and wanted to get on. Because I didn't want a ride, Uncle Hughie turned the horse around and rode back to the station house.

Sally

Sally was a calf that belonged to one of the teachers. She tried to eat Dotty's dress down by the chook yard, and the missionaries had to get the dress out of her mouth. Surprisingly, Sally didn't put any holes in the dress.

Long after Sally had grown up and been sent away, we were woken up one night by a loud noise – a cow was stuck in our doorway! The kids on the bottom bunks jumped onto the top bunks. Everyone was screaming and crying. The boys pulled the cow back through the door and shooed it away. We thought Sally had come home to be with us, but she had grown too big to fit through the door.

good with the bad

I remember when Uncle Yami Lester was in the AIM Hospital at Oodnadatta. When he was only a teenager, he was affected by the Maralinga bomb blasts. Black clouds came across the land, and it turned out they were from atomic tests. The explosions hurt Uncle Yami's eyes, and he had been blind ever since. A lot of people were affected by what happened at Maralinga – many died. Two girls in the mission also had sore eyes.

When the missionaries let us visit Uncle Yami, the boys tried to pull his bandage off to see his eyes. They thought he would be able to see who was talking to him.

Uncle Yami Lester became a famous Aboriginal leader. Even though he was blind, he stood up for Aboriginal people and land rights. He spoke up for Anangu people to look after language and culture, and he campaigned for Aboriginal people affected by the Maralinga bombs. He was Yangkunytjatjara like me.

Christmas

One Christmas, there was a party at the hospital clinic. Father Christmas arrived on a camel-drawn cart. The community had sent gifts for the kids, and Father Christmas was waving and calling out, 'Ho Ho Ho! Merry Christmas!' The missionaries had never told us about Father Christmas, so we guessed they were cross when we were given presents from this man dressed in red-and-white. He was not in our Bible stories.

When we got back to the mission, our presents were put on shelves and covered up with a large cloth. We never saw them again. We were confused by the whole thing.

chucking lollies

When the missionaries had lollies, they threw them in the air down near the laundry and the old classroom. Being one of the youngest, I got hardly any as everyone scrambled in the dirt like chooks. Peggy always shared her lollies with us younger ones.

the Ghan

The train-line was close to the mission, and we loved to watch the Ghan go past on its way to Oodnadatta Station. We travelled on the train once when we went to Adelaide for a holiday and saw the beach for the first time. We sat in the last carriage – the one reserved for Aboriginal people. As the train chugged along, we looked out at the purple-and-blue daisies and the yellow wattles growing along the track.

punishments

If we accidentally ripped our clothes when we were playing, we had to wear hessian potato sacks with cut-out holes for our head and arms. This happened to me and the girls if we played chasey and ran through the barbed wire fence next to the yard and tore our dresses. The missionaries thought we had deliberately done it. The potato sacks were so itchy that we couldn't play. We just sat on drums or the long seats on the verandah. Sometimes, the other kids got sad and sat with the ones wearing sacks.

If someone did something wrong, though not really bad, and didn't own up, we all had to line up for a spoonful of mustard. Nobody likes mustard in their mouth because it burns. We couldn't keep it in and would have this curry-coloured mixture dribbling from our mouths. We would get it on our clothes.

Racing
Racing
KJM

If the missionaries thought we were not listening, we could be sent to the corner to stand with our hands behind our backs. You might be there for a whole day, or even have to go back the next day. We didn't always understand what they were saying, so sometimes we lied to get out of trouble. If we were found out, we were punished.

nanju tjuta

There was no toilet paper – just pieces of newspaper. One time, all the newspaper blew out of the toilet into the mission yard, and someone yelled that there were nanju tjuta (horses) galloping. We girls were excited to see pictures of horses, and we pretended they were racing each other. Sister Bullpit got mad and came out with a big stick. We didn't know the pictures were from the horse-racing pages. We couldn't even read or write so how were we to know they were to do with gambling?

colourful clothes

We loved the colourful second-hand clothes that came into the mission, and it was a way for all the mothers to come to see us. They would pick out dresses they liked and wear them on top of one another. Sometimes, they were wearing four or five dresses when they left. The women got second-hand clothes as payment for working at the mission – washing clothes in the trough, hanging out clothes to dry, or washing floors.

This is one of the favourite memories I like to paint. I loved all those bright colours, and it made our families really happy.

McInerney
Box.
McInerney
McInerney
Box
McInerney
Box
McInerney
Box
KJM

leaving the Children's Home

I was washing my sheet rags one day and noticed cardboard boxes outside the visitors' house with the name 'McInerney' written on them. Why were there boxes with our names on them? I knew that something was going to happen. I wondered if we were going to be sent away, and I panicked. I was very worried.

moving away

On my last train ride out of Oodnadatta, I didn't know whether my siblings and I would be going back to the Children's Home. The missionaries tricked my mother and told her we were going on a holiday. She had to sign papers but could not read what she was signing. They taught my mother to write her name 'Daisy'.

The women who were there to farewell their kids sang out, 'Kunyi, your mother is at the hospital gate waving to you.' A strange feeling came over me because I remembered those boxes with our names on them. I feared we wouldn't be coming back, and I didn't want to wave to my mother. The women insisted that I wave and go to the window to see her. I was nearly in tears. I felt upset with Robyn, my sister. She didn't know anything and was mucking around with the other kids – laughing and having fun. I told her to wave at our mother, but she wouldn't listen. I wouldn't look up either. I was too sad.

The missionaries were keeping an eye on us. I think they worked out that I knew we weren't coming back. My heart was heavy. I wanted to cry, but I didn't want to be told off for crying. I felt so alone and heavy-chested. I was about nine years old.

our mother's story

I was twenty-one when I found my mother again.
'Why didn't you come and look for us?' I asked her.
'I came down to Adelaide many times looking for you all, but they wouldn't let me see you,' she said. 'I'd work and work and get no money most times, but I always thought about you kids. Every day after my work, I went away from the station and sat under a gum tree – first one tree and then another – and I just cried for you kids.'

Nine children altogether were taken away from my mother and sent to Adelaide. Some were adopted by non-Aboriginal families, and the rest stayed with non-Aboriginal foster families. I was fostered and had to stay with that family until I was seventeen.

My mother had twelve children – some died and the rest of us were taken away. She would cry every day, worrying about us, wondering where we were, and if we were safe and looked after. She wanted so much to see us, but that could not be. Some of my siblings never saw her again.
My mother died in her early fifties.

The U-shapes on the ground by her fingers are all her children.

KJM

With Thomas and Robyn not long after we arrived at the Children's Home in 1955.

Pushing Thomas on the mission swing. Robyn and I are holding the poles.

In front of the water tank — Robyn and Thomas are sitting and I'm behind them at the end. Baby Michael's in the back on the left.

Picnic at Hookey's Hole — I'm at the back and Thomas is in the middle. Robyn's on the left.

Out on the ute — that's Tjumi in front and Peggy's holding Thomas.

Waiting for our last train ride out of Oodnadatta.

In Adelaide with Thomas, Michael, and Robyn. This photo was taken before we knew we were going to be split up from the other kids at the Children's Home.

Visiting Granny Tjandi when I was older.

When I was artist-in-residence at Flinders University Art Museum, 1992

Kunyi June Anne McInerney was born on Todmorden Station near Oodnadatta in South Australia in 1950. Her family's language group is Yankunytjatjara. When Kunyi was four years old, she and three of her siblings were taken from their family to live at the Oodnadatta Children's Home. At the Children's Home, Kunyi was renamed Anne. Five years later, she was sent away again. This time to a foster family in Adelaide who called her June.

Kunyi became a nurse and midwife. She later graduated with a BA in Aboriginal Studies (University of SA). Kunyi has painted throughout her life, and her work has been exhibited widely. The paintings in *Kunyi* were part of the 'My Paintings Speak for Me' exhibition at the Migration Museum, a selection of which toured South Australia. Kunyi has illustrated several children's picture books.

Kunyi's paintings and stories are a moving testament to the Stolen Generation and the Children's Home kids she called family.

Acknowledgements

I acknowledge my Yankunytjatjara people from whom I was taken away.

This book is for all the Children's Home kids who were a part of these stories. Over the years, Tjumi Yvonne Johnson and I have talked for hours about our experiences. I want this book to be something we all can be proud of and which will help us heal together.

Thank you to Professor Vincent Megaw who started my artist career as artist-in-residence at Flinders University Art Museum.

Thank you to Fernando Galnaves for photographing the paintings.

Special thanks to Maggie Fletcher, who encouraged me to paint my stories with support from Arts SA. Maggie curated my exhibition 'My Paintings Speak for Me' with the Migration Museum, worked with Magabala Books, and did so much else inbetween.

And thank you to my children. I'm telling my stories for them. Kamara spent many hours writing up my stories for me. When my daughter Yaritji was little, she said 'I didn't grow up in a home. I grew up in an art gallery!' And now my son, Ribnga, works in an art gallery.

This is a Magabala Book

LEADING PUBLISHER OF ABORIGINAL AND
TORRES STRAIT ISLANDER STORYTELLERS.

CHANGING THE WORLD, ONE STORY AT A TIME.

First published 2021
Magabala Books Aboriginal Corporation
1 Bagot Street, Broome, Western Australia
Website: www.magabala.com
Email: sales@magabala.com

Magabala Books receives financial assistance from the Commonwealth Government through the Australia Council, its arts advisory body. The State of Western Australia has made an investment in this project through the Department of Local Government, Sport and Cultural Industries. Magabala Books would like to acknowledge the generous support of the Shire of Broome, Western Australia.

Magabala Books is Australia's only independent Aboriginal and Torres Strait Islander publishing house. Magabala Books acknowledges the Traditional Owners of the Country on which we live and work. We recognise the unbroken connection to traditional lands, waters and cultures. Through what we publish, we honour all our Elders, peoples and stories, past, present and future.

Paintings in *Kunyi* are acrylic on canvas except for 'Bath Time', oil on canvas.

Cover and Internal Design Jo Hunt
Printed and bound by Everbest Printing Ltd

ISBN 9871925936 57 5

A catalogue record for this book is available from the National Library of Australia

McInerney
Box 6